CW00329153

'In this tale of loneliness, tr
words provides a seam of li
Johnston's conception of words as making journeys
through history like refugees, survivors in strange
lands.'

Sally-Anne Lomas, author of *Live Like Your Head's On
Fire*

Source

A Saga

Rosemary Johnston

**Story
Mach\ne**

Source, Copyright © Rosemary Johnston, 2021

Print ISBN: 9781912665105
Ebook ISBN: 9781912665112
Published by Story Machine, 130 Silver Road, Norwich, NR3 4TG; www.storymachines.co.uk

Set in Garamond; used under licence.

Printed and bound in the UK by Seacourt Ltd

Story Machine is committed to the environment.
This book is printed using processes that are:

100%	100%	100%	100%	100%	100%	Zer0 % waste
carbon positive	EMAS	renewable energy	ISO14001	eco-friendly simitri® toner	recycled FSC® stock	

Printed by **seacourt** – proud to be counted amongst the top environmental printers in the world

Source

A Saga

In memory of my father, William Johnston

The time had come to clear out the old family farm. Both Kate's parents had now died, her father some time ago and her mother just last year. Out of a sense of duty - and little else - Kate had returned for her mother's funeral. She had arrived just in time for the service and, not wanting any condolences, hadn't hung around afterwards. The place had been empty since then. But in recent months, the house and its possessions had, in Kate's mind, begun to seem tinged with the resentment of having no purpose. So she had started planning to clear the house and sell it.

Someone might come and renovate the house. But a buyer would more likely want to knock it down and start again - she'd overheard a neighbour at the funeral mention that giant black slugs had invaded the roof space. The buyer would probably turn the semi wild bogland into a garden that would look unnaturally suburban in this landscape of strewn boulders.

So Kate had come back to the west of Ireland accompanied by her daughter, Lavinia, who was as unfitting as a landscaped garden in the Connemara wilderness with her Jack Wills coat and her Uggs.

They entered the whitewashed farmhouse through the kitchen, Lavinia complaining about the lack of signal and asking where the shops were. The place seemed in darkness even though it was the middle of an April day. Kate fumbled around for the light switch. She could see that someone else must have tidied away the tea things. The drying cloths were still where the neighbours had hung them over the handle on the oven door when the last of the mourners had left, the wedding-present crockery having fulfilled its last function.

'God!' said Lavinia, looking down at the flagged floor of the kitchen. 'Look at this place!' Kate watched her take in the kitchen table with its floral oil cloth and the old stone sink, underneath which was a cupboard, fronted by a curtain. She walked over to a painted dresser which stood at one end of the kitchen like the old matriarch in her tattered sage green apron. For years before her mother's death, Kate had almost taken pleasure in thinking of the day when she would be able to take the shelves full of ornaments and just throw them away. The sandwich plates, the soup tureen and the solitary ladle hanging from a hook. She couldn't imagine that anyone had come to eat at the house for years anyway. But now that the day was here, it was not pleasure she felt, more the assuagement that might be found in an ending.

Kate set down on the table a shopping bag containing the basic provisions they'd acquired at the airport. Then she dragged a suitcase to the living room which adjoined the kitchen. There was an open fireplace and a black leather sofa covered with a crocheted blanket that these days would be called a throw.

'It's freezing!' cried Lavinia.

'There's storage heaters. I'll put them on, but they'll take a while to get going.'

'What's that smell?' asked Lavinia, sniffing.

'Damp. I'll open the windows, get some fresh air moving round the place.'

'Are we really going to sleep here?'

'Why not?'

'It's mouldy.'

'Oh! I thought you meant because of the ghosts!' said Kate.

'Mum!'

'It'll do you good to experience a bit of hardship.'

Not knowing what state the bedding would be in, Kate had filled a suitcase with sleeping bags and pillows. She unpacked them now and followed Lavinia along the hallway, passing the bathroom and her mother's bedroom, to the room that had been Kate's.

She waited on the threshold while Lavinia nosied around, bending down under the sloping ceiling to peer through the low set draughty window.

Someone had stripped the single bed and placed the folded bedding on the chest of drawers.

'Where will you sleep?' Lavinia asked.

Looking back to her mother's room, the door firmly shut, Kate nodded to the living room, 'I'll have the sofa.'

She passed the sleeping bag and a pillow to Lavinia.

'Are you sure? What about granny's room?'

She shook her head. The door to that room would stay shut for at least today.

Kate returned to the kitchen and unpacked the groceries. She handed a loo roll to Lavinia who took it with her into the bathroom. She unravelled the other sleeping bag over the sofa and set about taking the necessary items from the case.

'There's no lock on the bathroom door,' said Lavinia.

Kate had wondered, before they left England, to what extent Lavinia's presence or innocent observations would push Kate to disclose, or simply to remember. But for now, she just hesitated before replying.

'It doesn't really matter, there's only us two.' Kate took a roll of bin bags from the suitcase. 'We might as well get started. The sooner we start the sooner we finish.'

'What's the plan?'

'I suppose most of it will just get thrown away.'

'Won't that make you sad?'

'No. I said goodbye to it all a long time ago.'

Kate took a bag and started filling it with china shepherdesses from the mantelpiece, string and buttons from drawers in the dresser, watching Lavinia as she took out the twenty or so books that were in a small book-case.

'Keep that book,' said Kate.

'What is it?' asked Lavinia.

'Poetry. Patrick Kavanagh.'

'Did granny like poetry?'

'No, she never read anything. It was your grand-dad's book. There's a dictionary somewhere. Keep that as well.'

Kate took the book from her fair haired, freckled daughter. She looked through its thick, mildewed pages for the poem that had been her first introduction to grown up poetry, many years ago. She could almost see her younger self, sitting cross legged and hesitant in front of the bookcase, not sure if it was permitted or not, to read grown up poetry.

Her father had found her there and asked what she was reading.

'Ah!' he said 'Kavanagh! Great choice.' And he opened the book and started to read:

On Raglan Road on an autumn day

I met her first and knew
That her dark hair would weave a snare
That I might one day rue.

He gave her back the book and said 'We should pay more heed to the poets.'

At the time Kate had taken it as a general piece of advice.

'He liked poetry and history and languages,' Kate said. 'The things he loved I came to love.'

'How did they meet?' asked Lavinia.

'He came to Connemara on the back of his friend's motor bike. It was to the wedding of a cousin of his friend. Granny was there. Love at first sight. He wooed her with the poetry and all that.'

'Is this what you wanted?' asked Lavinia, handing an old book to Kate.

'Yes, that's it. It's his dictionary.'

Despite Kate's claim that the objects in the house would provoke no sentiment, holding the dictionary filled her with that empty feeling that loss could fire at you; clearly the person who had made use of the book was no longer here to do so.

'It's very precious.'

'That old thing?' Lavinia held her hand across her mouth. 'That smell. It's making me gag.'

'You don't need to be so dramatic about it,' said Kate, smelling the book. But it was true, the book was musty, as if all the old words had gone off a bit, unused and trapped inside. Let us out! they might whisper. And the words in it might well be the key to unlocking the past. But the odour the trapped words gave off seemed to hold within it an accusation that it was the past itself that was tainted, no matter which words were chosen to describe it. Kate set the book down.

'When's it going to warm up?' asked Lavinia.

Rain was starting to pelt on the windowpanes. The room darkened as if night was drawing in.

'Tomorrow…. maybe.'

'Tomorrow? Can we light the fire?'

The ashes lay in the grate from the last time it had been lit.

'We can't! I don't know what state the chimney is in. It might be full of birds' nests, then the room would fill up with smoke. Your granny always liked the fire. The hearth and her kinfolk, that was all she wanted, really.'

Kate was about to say that in French the word for hearth and the word for home were the same word, 'foyer', and wasn't that interesting, but then Lavinia asked:

'What's for dinner?'

And Kate decided to keep the thought to herself.

'It'll have to be the pub. I can't cook here.'

'What sort of food does it have?'

'You like sushi don't you?'

'Yes! They have sushi?'

'Well, you might get lucky, but I doubt it!'

◆

In the pub, Lavinia picked snobbily through her plate of Irish stew and watched in disbelief at the way a tall man with dark eyes and greying hair stood at the bar and drank himself into oblivion. When he was about to keel over the other men at the bar reached out their arms and caught him, as if a nightly reflex. He was so thin, he might snap in two as he fell.

'Why does the landlord let him drink so much? They wouldn't allow that in London.'

'Perhaps here they know why he needs to drink.'

Later on, they walked back in the darkness. The wind was blowing off the sea, driving the rain into their faces. There were no street lights. A shape loomed up in front of them. For a moment it looked like a great black bull. Kate stopped in a panic and thought about throwing herself into the ditch to avoid it. But as the shape became more distinct she realised it was a couple struggling to keep hold of a big black umbrella.

◆

The next morning, while Kate waited for Lavinia to wake up, she picked up the old dictionary and looked through it. It was one of her dad's few possessions, the dictionary, that and the other books in the bookcase that he'd brought with him when he'd moved into the farm. The bond that had developed between Kate and her dad because of their interest in its contents, made the book all the more cherished.

Looking through it now, she thought how there were many words in her father's dictionary that had fallen out of use. But the words no longer included in dictionaries of today still existed somehow even if the thing they were describing had become obsolete. And there were many words that had come in to use since her father's dictionary had been printed. Words to do with new inventions or concepts, but not just those. As the world changed, the words to describe it changed. Language was endlessly renewing itself. Some words were completely new, or new to English, but even words for new inventions did not necessarily have newly invented words assigned to them. Many were just adapted from words already in existence. As if language was a cuckoo using another bird's nest.

Lavinia came into the kitchen carrying her iPad and sat down at the table, sleepy eyed.

Kate set about making strong tea, boiled in the teapot on top of the cooker for old time's sake, and placed a packet of Jaffa Cakes down in front of Lavinia.

'Is that it?' Lavinia asked.

'I was just thinking I would take the dictionary back to show my ESL students.'

'I'm sure they'll love that.'

'It's a lovely day. Let's go for a walk when you're ready. All this old stuff can wait.'

But the old stuff couldn't wait and followed them as they descended the lane towards a bungalow. Beyond the bungalow in the grey choppy sea, islets appeared to sway, like unsteady mirages.

They passed some fields in one of which lay the remains of an old cart.

'There used to be some donkeys in that field,' said Kate. 'There's a photo of me somewhere on one of them. The donkey is being pulled on a rope by the boys who lived here. Two brothers.'

The gorse in the lane blazed bright yellow and spikey.

'After they were married,' said Kate, 'granddad was supposed to help on the farm. All your granny's family were very welcoming to him. But he had no interest in farming. He was a city boy really.'

'Could he not teach if he was into all that, books and stuff?'

'He had no qualifications. That was what was different about him, to be a working-class man and interested in culture and so on.'

By now they had reached the shore and they walked along the water's edge, through the blowing sand.

The drunk man from the pub was a little way ahead of them, tinkering with an upturned rowing boat.

He turned round and looked at Kate and Lavinia, nodded in acknowledgement.

'Does he recognise us from the pub?'

'He's more likely to recognise me from thirty years ago.'

'Do you know him?'

'I used to know him. His name is Brian.'

Kate thought about going over to him but wasn't sure if he would welcome her approach. She sat on a damp rock and looked out to sea. She wished she could have a cigarette, that she could have one day off from giving up, that she could sit and inhale the smoke and the little high would somehow simultaneously intensify and anaesthetise her emotions at being back in this place.

'Oh!' cried Lavinia. 'I've got sand all over my Uggs.'

Brian was getting ready to put his boat in the water but, hearing Lavinia's voice, he turned to look at them, hesitated before making his way over to them.

'Are you back for a while?' he asked.

'Just clearing out the farm.'

'Oh aye!'

'Mum died.'

'That was a while ago.'

Kate nodded.

'I heard you were back for the funeral, but then you disappeared.'

'It's a bit hard to….'

Brian nodded.

'Mine died, too.'

'I'm sorry.'

'Sometimes a dead mother is no bad thing.'

'Do you think so?' Kate stifled a sob.

'Will you put it up for sale?'

'Probably.'

'Another holiday cottage it'll become.'

'Do you think the chimney is safe enough for us to light the fire?'

'Oh I don't know. There's been water coming into that little building for a while. The brickwork, I don't know.'

'Lavinia here is a pampered puss from the big smoke. She's feeling the cold.'

'She's the image of you.'

'She's a bit too interested in fashion to be my image. And I'm not sure if fashion and deep thinking go together.'

'Are you still into thinking, Kate?'

'It never stops.'

'I've found a way to make it stop.'

'I know. I saw you last night.'

He nodded in acknowledgement.

'We can talk later if you want,' said Kate. 'You can buy me a drink.'

'I'll buy you a drink for sure, but there'll be no talking. I have to catch the tide. I'll call up at the farm later.'

◆

'That man!' said Lavinia as they walked up the lane towards the farm. 'Who would say that.... dead mothers...'

'Now you can begin to see why I don't come back!'

'Was he your boyfriend?'

'Well, no, well yes, well, sort of, no, not really.'

'Why not?'

'I don't think he was really interested in girls.'

'Is he gay?'

'I don't mean that. I mean, he was only interested in being out of his head, even then.'

They passed a modern house with a large sliding window which overlooked the coastline. It didn't seem right and jarred with Kate's memory of a ramshackle farm with deep windows cut into the stone.

'It was all small farms that just about managed their existence and people who lived in them generation after generation. Like granny's place. Now it's all holiday homes.'

'Who lived here then?'

Kate started to laugh. 'I'm not sure I can tell you.'

'Why?'

'Dark secrets from the past.'

'Mum! The internet – there are no more secrets in the world.'

'Can you handle Cup-a-Soup for lunch?'

'Mum, for God's sake, I'm going to DIE of starvation!'

'Sure you're always on a diet.'

They supplemented their lunch with more Jaffa Cakes and mugs of tea, Lavinia shivering under the crocheted blanket.

'When's your boyfriend going to turn up?'

'He'll be hours out at sea.'

'What's he doing out there? Is he fishing?'

'Fishing is a sort of pretext.'

'What do you mean?'

'He's looking for something.'

'What?'

It wasn't the right time for explanations, so Kate just said

'Whatever it is he is looking for at night at the bottom of the whiskey bottle he's looking for by day out on the water.'

'God!' said Lavinia and she put her headphones on and started singing.

◆

From outside came the rattling noise of a pair of ladders being put up.

A few minutes later, Brian stepped into the house. He barely spoke as he knelt down in front of the fire and peered up the chimney.

Kate and Lavinia watched as he hung a filthy sheet in front of the fire and instructed Kate to hold onto it. Outside, he climbed up the ladders carrying a long brush. Soot came down the chimney followed by a long dead blackbird.

A few minutes later he stepped back into the house.

He took the cloth from Kate and peered back up the chimney.

'It looks ok, you can light the fire. Have you got enough turf?'

'I think there might be some in the shed.'

He turned to go.

'Where are you living these days?' asked Kate.

'Back at the bungalow.'

Seeing a line of bin bags, he asked 'What are you going to do with those?'

'Is it even worth driving twenty miles along a country road to the charity shop? A skip might be a better idea.'

'I'll bring the truck round in a day or two and get rid of them all in one go for you.'

Even after all this time he seemed to understand her.

Lavinia looked up from her iPad for a moment and took her headphones off.

'Mum? I want to email dad. Where can I get a signal? Do they have wifi at the pub?'

'You could always ask............but they might laugh at you.'

'Mum!'

Brian and Kate laughed.

'Go to the hotel.' said Brian. 'I'll give you a lift if you want.'

'No, it's ok,' said Lavinia, slightly panicked 'I'll walk up there.'

She put on her coat and took her iPad and as she walked out of the door, Kate called 'Don't forget to

check out the Spa!' Brian looked at Kate and laughed
but then a split second later, he too walked out of the
farm. Kate had the strong impression he didn't want to
be alone with her.

◆

A few days later, still sifting and sorting, the number of
bin bags growing. Lavinia picked up a photo of her
mother, a freckled child with flaxen hair, kneeling on a
beach with a bucket and spade. She was smiling at
whoever was taking the photo.

'I never knew you belonged to this place. I always
thought of you in London.'

'Does it make a difference?' asked Kate.

'You used to belong somewhere else. You had
another life before me.'

'That's true.'

'Why did we never come here? Did you not miss
granny?'

Kate thought for a moment about how she'd missed
her mother, the way she used to be, the mother she was
smiling at in the photo, and not the one she had become.
So she said 'I missed my homeland.'

'Your homeland?'

'Homeland is like the birthplace of your soul. It's
not just a country. It's the colour of the hedgerows, the
cry of a curlew…. the way neighbours greet you.'

'Did you ever bring me?'

'I came a few times over the years but it always ended up in the same argument so I'd decided to stop coming long before I had you.'

'What did you argue about?'

'She wanted me to be something I wasn't and I refused to be it.'

'What did she want you to be?'

'She wanted me to be her.'

Kate thought about her mother's desire to keep Kate on the farm, to marry a local boy and have children and perpetuate the thing all over again. She didn't want to accept her mother's limitations. Now that she was hovering above the past like a keen-eyed kestrel, Kate could see that her mother was trying to make her life work again, a second chance, through Kate.

'What did you want?'

'I wanted to be myself.'

'That's funny,' said Lavinia.

'What's funny about it?'

'You don't have to want to be yourself. You just are.'

'That was the essence of our arguments, Lavinia, dear. I just was myself, no point in trying to be any other. But granny tried.'

Kate shivered at the memory of their arguments, like boxing matches.

'What about granddad?'

'He wanted me to be free.'

'That's funny, too.'

'I suppose he wanted to be free, too.'

'Free from what?'

'From granny.'

'Why?'

'I think it turned out to be a sort of holiday romance. He was always out, tramping the hills à la recherche de something or other.'

'What do you mean?'

'He was drawn by the loneliness of this place and then he found it wasn't enough. He would go away for a while, looking for other types of work, and then come back. He was restless.'

'Did granny mind?'

'She was mortally embarrassed. For granny and her family the land was everything to them, their livelihood, their home as it had been for generations. She'd fallen for this outsider, her family had been kind to him, but then he didn't work the land or belong to it. He just visited.'

And then the conflict, for Kate, that she still loved this man that her mother was starting to hate. And then her mother's anger, that made it harder for her father to come back. And that if he came back, it was to Kate, not to her mother.

'Did you never see him again?'

'I did, but it was like an affair, carried out in secret.'

'That's a bit funny.'

'It wasn't.'

'Where did you see him, when he came back?'

'At his girlfriend's.' Kate giggled.

'Granddad had a girlfriend? No way!' Lavinia laughed.

'I think he had a few,' Kate smiled. 'One of them lived down there by the sea, that new house.'

'That house with the big windows?'

'On that land, yes. But not that house. It was a little farm then with little windows. No matter the size of the windows, your granny still knew what was going on inside.'

◆

Kate took some papers from a pile by the sofa to build a fire. She lifted the dark turf she'd brought in from the shed and hoped it would light. Her mother had never liked the fire to go out.

She picked up the dictionary that was lying on the floor beside Lavinia's iPad.

'This dictionary was to me like your iPad is to you. It was the source of all my knowledge.'

'I'm glad I didn't live here then. The only thing to do to look up words in the dictionary. How boring!'

'One day' said Kate, 'I wanted to know how to spell a word. Dad showed me how the dictionary could help me work it out.'

Lavinia picked up her iPad and started tapping at the screen.

'He told me that in the dictionary you could find out not only how to spell a word but also what the word meant and where the word had come from. Well, he was teaching me about etymology, though I didn't know that then.'

On hearing the word 'etymology', Lavinia picked up her earphones.

'Looking up that word set me on a course. That was the beginning of my love of words and languages.'

Lavinia put the earphones on. She didn't share Kate's interest in either the past or in words.

Her father had looked around the room and said, 'Let's look up a word.' He chose the word 'window'.

'Let's see what we can learn,' he had said.

He turned over the pages in the dictionary until they found the word and then he showed her it had come from Old Norse. Kate didn't know what that meant.

'It's a Viking word,' her father explained.

How could that be, that the word had travelled all this way, through all those years?

She remembered her father reading from the dictionary, in those days before he had been unable to bear living there, his voice softly insistent with its own particular inflection.

'A "wind eye"', he said 'and isn't that a perfect description of a window if ever there was one.'

The memory of his voice moved her, like a song he was singing to teach her, like a ballad, like a love song. She couldn't get enough of it.

So much for mother tongue, thought Kate. In this house, the gift of language came from her father.

He told Kate they should make a collection of Viking words every time they came across one. She was still collecting them. Window, freckle, bairn, anger, birth, bleak, guest, haunt, snare. You might even be able to make a sentence that consisted just of Viking words.

When Kate and her father sat inside, looking through the dictionary together, her mother was often outside with the livestock, working. Sometimes Kate would see her mother look in at them. In those days, Kate had been inward looking and her mother's thoughts were always of the outside but that had gradually shifted and later Kate's view turned outwards and her mother's inwards. The dictionary had fuelled Kate's inner life and was her way of getting to the root of all things but it was also her future and her means of escape later, when her mother became as dark as peat.

'Mum, do you mind if I walk up to the hotel with my iPad?' asked Lavinia.

'No, ok.'

'If I can get a signal, I'll watch a film or something so I might be a while.'

Lavinia stood up and put on her jacket with its dramatically large fur trimmed hood. She tied her hair up in a messy bun.

'I'll email dad and download some more music. OK? I've listened to all the songs I've got too many times.'

'Off you go.'

What would be Lavinia's connection to the world? Her mother had the land, that was everything for her and for Kate it was words. Not fashion, surely, or technology? How would that 'earth' you or give the world meaning?

Kate's interest in words was as incomprehensible to Lavinia as Lavinia's interest in fashion was to Kate, as Kate's interest in words had been incomprehensible to her mother, as her mother's interest in the land had been to Kate. That was ok. A mother and a daughter – they are not one and the same.

Kate went into the kitchen and rummaged through the drawers of the old dresser. She found what she was looking for – a notebook that had probably been there since Kate had been at school.

She took it to the sofa and sat with a pen and the dictionary, looking through it to build a list of Viking words. She could imagine that some of the children she taught might enjoy them. What fun they would have making a sentence from words like 'husband', 'ugly' and 'blunder'.

Migrants were like word-importers, anyway. The older students might appreciate the idea of themselves being part of a bigger picture. They were living proof of the movement of language. Whatever the impetus that set them on their journey: economic need, war, hunger or just a desire for discovery or escape, some of the words migrants brought would escape their homes out into the streets and cities of the new country. They would bend and alter and become assimilated, like the migrants themselves. There was no such thing as a pure language. Every language was a mix of other languages. Words were very flexible. It is probably what enabled them to endure for centuries or even millennia. They metamorphose, thought Kate, causing a kind of word-spawning, which leaves behind cocoons that contain enough similarity to be just about recognisable - word-shells, which develop their own meaning and purpose.

◆

Lavinia returned a couple of hours later, flushed and invigorated.

'There's going to be a concert at the hotel on Saturday,' she said. 'Can I go?'

'Ok. I'll come along with you. A night out'd be great.'

'No.' said Lavinia, surprisingly emphatic. 'It's not your sort of thing, it's not folk, it's more… urban.'

Kate looked up at Lavinia.

'OK,' she said. 'Did you email your dad?'

'Yes.'

'Is he missing us?'

'Well, he didn't exactly say that.'

They both laughed.

'Next time we come can we stay there? Can we go and eat there? They've got tempura prawns on the menu.'

Tempura prawns!

◆

She'd had three or four glasses of wine. Well, ok, maybe five.

Kate and Lavinia were walking back from the hotel in the dark along the melancholy road. Lavinia had got her wish to have prawns for dinner. It had not gone unnoticed by her mother that Lavinia had spent most of the evening chatting to a barman.

'Brian and his brother, they loved their boat. They were always in it or tinkering with it. But they also liked to drink.'

On each side of the road in the distance were the lights from the farmhouses and cottages. The sea in the distance sounded at peace.

'One day,' said Kate 'Brian returned alone, rowing furiously and dragging the boat up the beach shouting for help, that Kieron had fallen overboard. People came running and took over the boat from Brian. He was shouting and trying to get back in the boat, but they wouldn't let him. He kicked off his boots and started to swim. Someone got in the water and dragged him back.'

'Did they find him?'

'Brian was running along the shore, water pouring off him, shivering, shouting Kieron's name.'

Kate groped around her empty pockets for the reassurance of a packet of cigarettes. She imagined lighting up and inhaling.

'They came back in after an hour or so. If he wasn't to be found then, he wouldn't be found alive.'

'God, mummy! This place is completely grim.'

'His body washed up a few days later further down the coast. The funeral was at the church there.'

Kate could hardly bring herself to remember. All the teachers from their school had attended the funeral so the school had closed for the day.

'Brian's mother was half demented with grief. Crying and shouting on the steps of the church. She blamed Brian. Accused him of throwing the boy overboard'

'Did he?'

'No one knows what really happened. But no doubt there was booze involved and maybe a bit of messing around…. Those boys…. alcohol was a part of their lives from a young age. I don't know where that hurt began, somewhere far back.'

They were back at the farm now. The fire was still alight and some of the chill had gone.

Lavinia went straight to bed, hardly uttered goodnight.

Poor child, thought her mother. I am overwhelming my pampered pooch with the darkness of the old days.

Kate gave the fire a good poke and put more turf on it. She wanted to open the bottle of wine she had brought from the hotel but of course! Her teetotal mother! No corkscrew! She took a screwdriver from the drawer instead and with it and a bash from the rolling pin, she managed to push the cork into the bottle which it did with an upward surge of the cheap wine from within. Never mind! There was wine! She poured it into a mug and drank. It gave her no pleasure, the bitter wine, like vinegar. She spat out the miniscule pieces of cork that had ended up in the mug.

'Fuck!' she thought, what was this place doing to her, sending her spiralling back to the old days, packets of cigarettes, pints of wine.

But she drank it all down anyway, the first mugful then another.

She was remembering waiting outside the church, watching the funeral procession from across the road. She didn't want to go inside. The little church was named after St Brendan, the patron saint of sailors. The ceiling of the chancel was carved in wood in the form of an upturned boat. That would have been nice for his mother, thought Kate, when she lifted her eyes to heaven looking for succour, to be reminded each time of the cause of her torment.

Everyone else was at the service. Except Brian. His mother had been too angry and wouldn't let him attend. God knows what conversations had taken place before the funeral to try to convince her that it wasn't Brian's fault and to exclude him would be the wrong thing to do. But that is what she did. One son had died and the other had been negligent, if not responsible.

The coffin on the shoulders of the dark suited, dark haired men had entered the church. The sobbing started and rose up outside before the doors of the church were resolutely closed.

Out of nowhere Brian had appeared. He tried to open the doors.

The memory of it was too pitiful.

Kate drank another deep mouthful from the mug of wine.

She tried to push the memory away by putting more turf on the fire. She even picked up the book of Kavanagh and opened it but there was no way she was going to read tonight.

Brian had started to bang on the great wooden doors of the church, first with the cast iron rings, then with his palms and then with the whole length of his arms.

'Mummy,' he cried, 'let me in!'

Kate didn't know how the mourners inside could have borne to listen to it.

And then he started calling for his brother.

'Kieron!' he screamed 'Please! Let me in! Kieron!'

Screaming and weeping, he fell down on the steps in front of the church. He put his head between his knees and covered his sob-stained face with his hands. When he looked up, the cuts on his hands left bloody streaks on his hollow cheeks.

That was the end of him.

Kate could do no more than watch; the shrill howl of his grief made it impossible for her to approach him.

No one could.

And where did he go?

To the pub, of course.

Even now, Kate could still feel the church breathe its sigh of relief.

He would anaesthetise himself there in the pub on whiskey. And he would keep on anaesthetising himself there for the next thirty years.

Kate put the fireguard in front of the fire and slugged back the last of the wine. She slipped inside the sleeping bag and hoped for sleep.

◆

'Are you really going to see a band?' she asked Lavinia.

'Yes, why? Where else would I be going?'

◆

She'd told her mother she was going to see a band in the church hall and had walked off down the lane.

Her father had come back for one of his infrequent visits. He was staying with a woman, a Northerner who'd moved there to escape the Troubles and whose house was on the sea shore. Kate wasn't sure what sort of relation-ship they had.

Seeing him filled her with a deep longing that was

all the keener because of the certainty that the visit would be short lived. It was as if he had died and come back to life again. Or like the dream where the dead person returns to the living, with no questions asked or answered about where they have been or how long they might stay this time. The dream might presage hope. But Kate's father might die again. Not might - would. Each time he left was to lose him again. So there was an element of these visits that was unsettling. She had to see him, but that the meetings took place like this – furtive and fleeting, Kate blamed on her mother. Her loathing would permit no sensible arrangement. And neither Kate nor her father would dare risk the confrontation that would arise from such a discussion. So her mother stood, in Kate's mind, as the resolute obstruction that kept her from her father.

He asked her if she was still reading poems, and how was school and if she'd done ok in her exams and what she planned to do after. She told him she wanted to go and live in France and he said good, great, France is a great place to live. I'll come and live with you there. He'd been there once and he'd learned to say 'Voulez-vous vous promener avec moi ce soir, Mademoiselle?' Was she doing well in French at school? That was good, it was great to have a talent like that. He wished he could learn more. She told him they'd given her a book to read about a woman called Thérèse. She was enjoying reading about the pine forests of the south-west, where Thérèse lived. She'd like to go there one day and see what it was really like because it was difficult to imagine ever suffering from the oppressive heat, in Connemara. But she did understand the suffering she shared with Thérèse: the oppression of family, being forced into an ill-fitting role. And her desperation to escape even if the price was exile.

It was difficult to explain the book to her father, so she just said 'It's about a woman who hates her husband so much she tries to poison him.'

'Oh!' he said and looked alarmed and then Kate realised what she'd said.

'I miss you,' she said.

He put his arms around her. 'You know I can't live here. I've got myself a job in Cork. When I get my place sorted out you can come and stay.'

'Mummy is always in a bad mood since you left.'

'Is it money? I'll send you some when I can.'

'Always shouting at me. Because I got wet one day! Is it my fault that it rained?'

She started to sob.

'When you didn't like where you were living, you could just leave! But I can't leave yet! Where would I go?'

'Go for a walk til she calms down.'

'I told you I did! And it rained! And I got wet! And she shouted!'

The neighbour, aged in her forties, with dyed blond hair, was standing in the doorway, listening. Her mother would hate it if she knew.

'What have I done to make her so angry?'

If Kate's father knew the answer, he chose not to share it with Kate.

Now Kate was also angry. She took her coat and left. And where could she go now but back home so she strode up the lane between the hedgerows, tearful and indignant. Somewhere inside, Kate knew that her father was in part responsible for her suffering. But she tried hard to keep those feelings at bay, because he was the one she really loved.

When she reached the farmhouse, she stepped inside and crept towards her bedroom. Her mother sprang at her from behind the door of her own room.

'I saw where you went! You lied to me! That man! What's he doing staying in that house! And you visiting him there!' She almost growled.

Kate tried to walk past her but her mother stood in the way.

'He said he'll send you some money.'

'Money!' her mother screamed. 'He's talking about money? In that house with that woman! Right by the shore where everyone can see them!'

'Please mum! I just wanted to talk to him.'

'Every time I look out of my window now I'll see that house.'

'He's my dad.' Kate sobbed and tried to pass her mother.

'What sort of dad is he? He left you!' said her mother, blocking Kate's path and prodding her in the shoulder.

'He didn't leave me. He left you!'

'You two – you're both alike. Neither of you belong round here! With your books and your words, you think you're better than all this, the land. He used it 'til he needed it no more. You'll do the same.'

'I don't want to leave but it's the way you are that's giving me the idea.' Kate started to cry.

'You're not to see him again. Do you hear?'

Kate retreated to the bathroom. She'd taken to hiding out in there, sitting out her mother's rages now that she could no longer walk in the rain. She locked the door and paced the tiny room like a cell. This night was different, the rage would not subside. Her mother stood on the other side of the door shouting. She kept banging on the door, demanding that Kate should come out, come out, but Kate wouldn't, she couldn't face it, she kept hoping that her mother would just go away. Then the banging got louder, the door moving in its hinges.

There was a moment or two of silence then the shouting started up again.

'Come out! Come out!' her mother screamed. 'Come out now!'

Thump thump thump.

Kate's heart was thumping in her chest.

She could take no more. She opened the door.

Her mother was on the other side of the door, towering over Kate like a raging black bull.

In her hand she held a screwdriver.

'There'll be no more of that,' she said.

Her mother unscrewed the lock from the bathroom door.

She put the screwdriver and the lock on the windowsill of the little bathroom and they lay there for months, like the spoils of war.

◆

That night Kate ran down the lane to Brian's house.

She went round the back of the bungalow and knocked on the window.

'Brian,' she called. 'Open the window.'

He pulled back the curtain and opened the window and helped her climb in over the bed.

'That fucking woman. She's fucking mental!'

'Here' he said and handed her a cigarette. He sat down on his bed and smoked.

'I went to see my dad.'

'Your dad?'

'He's back for a couple of days. She went berserk! I thought she was going to break the door down.'

She lay down on the other bed.

'Fuck!' she said. 'Fuck!' She inhaled deeply.

Brian came and lay down beside her.

'Where's Kieron?' she asked.

'He's playing drums in the gig at the church hall. Mum and dad have gone to watch him.'

'When will they be back?'

'They'll be hours. By the time they pack up and brush ciggie butts off the floor and all that.'

Her head hurt. The more she thought, the worse it got. She couldn't go and live with her dad and she didn't want to live with her mother. She wanted to run away.

'Want to listen to some Springsteen?' Brian asked.

He got up and put the record on. There was only one song for this occasion and the words came out over the speakers.

Hey little girl is your daddy home?
Did he go away and leave you all alone.

'Brian, not this song,' she said. 'It's not funny.'

Then Brian took up a pretend mike and sang along.

Tell me now, baby, is he good to you?
And can he do to you the things that I do? Oh no
I can take you higher.
Oh! I'm on fire.

He came over and lay beside Kate and tried to kiss her while the song continued in the background.

'No' she said 'I don't need that sort of high. Have you got any blow? I need to get stoned. To get out of my head and not be here. He's right, your man, it's like a 6 inch knife in my skull and I need something for the pain.'

He rolled her a joint and they smoked and smoked until their throats were dry.

'Do you want to go to France?' she said.

'Yeah!' he said. 'Paris?'

'Paris,' she said. 'Montmartre…. Place de l'Opéra.'

Brian passed her the joint and she took a drag.

'Or – I know!' she said. 'We could go to Argelouse. See if we could find Thérèse.'

'Who's that?'

'She's from the book we're reading.'

She passed him back the joint and he dragged on it.

'So we're going to go to France to find some woman from a fucking book?'

'I bet she'd have some decent wine, Thérèse.'

They started to giggle but their laughter was false and petered out to silence.

The next morning the room smelled stale, of smoke and whiskey. Kieron lay comatose on his bed next to the window. Kate couldn't face Brian's parents, so she climbed over Kieron and out of the window and set off back home.

The houses round about were full of darkness and no matter how free the hills might seem, and the call of the sea and its idea of freedom, it wasn't that easy to get away.

The woman in the kitchen, her mother, had calmed down. There was no discussion, no apology but there was something almost regretful in her demeanour. Her head hung low over the frying pan when she cracked two eggs into it and fried them in silence.

She set a plate down on the table.

It wasn't breakfast that Kate needed.

What had happened to her mother? That laughing girl who'd relished collecting the banty eggs from the coop, where was she? Who'd hard boiled those eggs and mashed them up with mayonnaise and onion to make the sandwiches for a picnic. And packed them in a tartan shopping bag with a flask of tea and slices of honeydew melon and walked with her daughter along the lane with the hawthorn in bloom, to the beach where they spread the blanket out on the damp sand between the shoals of bladderwrack. Where had she gone that woman on those picnics? Because she had gone and she wouldn't be coming back. That woman who could no longer enjoy her view of the sea, her gaze turned away from life, her gaze turned away from the openness of life.

◆

Kate lay on the sofa listening for her daughter's key in the door but instead of a key she heard giggling. And a boy's voice.

Oh no. Then it went quiet.

That, in a way, was even worse.

◆

Kate picked up the notebook with the idea of adding to her notes about word-migration, enjoying the quiet stillness of the morning. She thought how when the words migrated, they changed, like people do. Some became more resilient, more powerful, some are lost by the wayside. Those Viking words were all carried around by humans. But words were also carriers, they were vessels, carrying our intentions, our needs and desires. Humankind has an influence on words but words also have the power to influence us. They are intertwined with the human experience. A symbiotic relationship. How would we do anything, thought Kate, it if were not for words. We needed to invent words in order to survive. And thrive. Language was an elemental part of evolution.

She heard Lavinia go into the bathroom, so she put the notebook to one side. She went into the kitchen and set about making some tea.

Lavinia came in and lay back on the sofa, her hair unbrushed, yawning.

Kate took her a cup of tea and sat down beside her.

'Late night?'

'Yeah.'

'I had an interesting night myself last night.'

'Oh? What did you get up to?'

'You first!' said Kate. 'Let's hear about the boy-friend!'

'He's not my boyfriend.'

'Is he in the band?'

'He does the lighting for them but he works at the hotel.'

'So that's why you've been spending all that time there! And here was me thinking you were very keen to keep in contact with your dad!'

Lavinia blushed.

'What's his name?'

'Enda.'

'Enda and Lavinia. Hmmm not sure that goes.....Do you Enda take thee Lavinia?'

'Mum!'

Both mother and daughter were in their pyjamas. Kate was feeling slightly groggy and thirsty.

'They asked if I want to sing with them sometime.'

'Who?'

'The band.'

'Oh.'

'Can we come back? We could do this place up a bit and stay here?'

'You've changed your tune. ...It sounds like a lot of work for a couple of weeks a year.'

Lavinia took out her nail polish from a brightly striped case and started painting her nails the same colour as the purple furry ankle length boots she wore for slippers.

'Everyone here really likes poetry.'

'I know.'

'It's a bit funny.'

'Does he write poetry, Enda?'

'How did you know?'

'Ah well!'

'He knew the poem, granddad's poem.'

'Oh.'

'He told me Van Morrison sang a version of it. Have you heard of him?'

Had she heard of Van Morrison?

'I downloaded it for you. Do you want to listen to it?'

'I've heard it before but I do want to hear it.'

Lavinia slipped down on to the rug in front of the fire. Kate joined her.

Lavinia reached over to the sofa to pick up her iPad. She saw Kate's notebook and picked it up and looked through the scrawl of Kate's handwriting.

'Are you writing poetry?'

'It's not poetry. Just some notes I made when I was thinking about dictionaries while you were gadding about with lover boy.'

Lavinia scrolled down her vast collection of music. Together they listened to Morrison's gruff northern voice sing 'On Raglan Road'.

'It's got a nice melody,' said Lavinia. She started to sing along.

Kate's head was full of the words. She knew the poem off by heart.

'Why don't you sing, mum?'

Kate was not so sure about singing along. She wanted to ask her daughter 'Do you think it is possible to just

39

sing your way out of your pain?'

She picked up the iPad and switched off the music.

'What are you doing, mum?' asked Lavinia.

'Sing it yourself.'

'Sing it myself?'

'Yes. You don't need the music.'

Kate lay back and listened to her daughter. When she started to sing the line about the quiet street where old ghosts meet, tears pricked Kate's eyes. Long ago, she had come to understand that the 'snare' from the poem that her father had referred to had been her mother. And what her mother had been suffering from was the shame of being unloved.

'You sing beautifully, Lavinia.' Kate was beginning to realise that Lavinia was taking the whole word thing to another level, adding music to it. And that words with music might be her child's way of making deep connections to the world.

'I used to put you on my knee when you were a tiny baby....'

'Oh God mum don't go there.'

'... and sing to you. I like to think I was passing on the gift of song to you. And you know, you used to sing back to me.'

'Yeah right!'

'You were listening to me and copying me. Little singing sounds came back to me. You were only eight weeks old.'

You didn't just give birth to a baby, Kate thought,

you give birth to a life and that life's vast potential. In Kate's case, her mother had given birth to her, but it had been her father who had given her her life. The definition of motherhood, thought Kate, was the nurturing of the acorn into the oak. Not to crush the acorn under the hoof of your bitterness.

Lavinia put the song back on. Morrison was now singing Kavanagh's line about walking 'the enchanted way.'

Thinking about 'the enchanted way' made Kate a bit worried.

'Did you walk the enchanted way last night?'

'Mum!'

'What?'

'You're not supposed to ask me questions like that.'

'Why not? Is it not in the rule book of mother and daughter conversations?'

'Anyway, I could ask you the same thing! Where were you last night anyway? What were you doing?'

'Lavinia dearest, I walked the enchanted way too often when I was young.'

'God, mum, you're so embarrassing!'

'It's better than being boring.'

Lavinia sighed deeply. 'I really like him.'

Oh God, her daughter was in love.

'I don't know if holiday romances work in this family,' said Kate.

If she wanted to have a relationship with this boy, it would mean that Kate would have to carry on having a relationship with this place. Did she want to? A couple of weeks here already had her thinking that she needed to go into therapy. And then last night…

'We could ask dad about a house in France. Put the pittance from this place towards buying somewhere over there.'

'Really?'

'Why don't you email your dad and ask him?'

'He'll think you've flipped.'

'Your dad has known me for twenty years. I'd flipped by the time we met.'

She thought for a few moments then said,

'Have you ever thought about a French boy? What about Jean Claude? Or Jean Luc. That's a nice name. I've heard that French boys are very good at enchantment. In fact it's a French word, I think. To do with singing! Perfect!'

'Mum!'

'Or how about Yannick, even? Yannick and Lavinia. That has a nice ring to it.'

'Mum!'

◆

What was she doing, really?

But she couldn't stop herself.

She knocked on the door of the bungalow.

Brian opened it. He looked at her for a moment before he let her in.

The house was in reasonable condition, in fact in some ways better than the farm, now in a state of chaos. It needed a lick of paint, no doubt, but there weren't the empty bottles everywhere that she had feared.

She was overwhelmed by a memory the moment she stepped inside, of Brian's teenage bedroom and their dope smoking binges. She'd spent evening after evening there with him, hiding, her refuge until Kieron's death.

Kate took her coat off, sat down, and looking around, asked,

'What was it like coming back to live here?'

'No different to anywhere else.'

'What do you mean?'

'He follows me around everywhere, I might as well have him back in his home.'

After Kieron's death, Brian had stayed at a relative's house, an arrangement which lasted about a week until they had had enough of his drunkenness. And so to another relative and then another. Or all day at the pub and then out into the street where sometimes he would fall down and lie there until someone picked him up and took him home. Sometimes he slept in his boat.

'Do you want a drink?'

'No, no thanks.'

Brian opened a can of Guinness and poured it into a glass. He sat down on the chair.

'How's life treated you all these years, Kate?'

'Pretty good,' she said, then 'eventually.'

'What are you up to these days?'

'Well, you met my daughter.'

Brian nodded.

'And I teach English to refugees.'

'Where are they from?'

'Anywhere there's a war, or strife. I love giving them the words, to help them find their new voice that'll help them live in their new country.'

Brian took a slug of his stout.

'Is it children? Or adults?'

'Both. It would be nice,' she continued 'if they could keep both sets of words but the younger ones don't always manage to. They lose their mother tongue. I feel a bit bad about that. Giving them something and taking something fundamental away at the same time. Helping them to lose their soul.'

She didn't know why she was telling him all this, except for him to know that in real time, everything was ok.

'But on the other hand, learning a second language allows them to live a second life. Which is great if the first life you had wasn't so good. Language is always thought of as allowing people to express themselves. And it is mostly a means to an end. It can be the bridge that helps you escape from a bad life to a better life. But really, it's much more than that. Language can be a way for you to triumph.'

Brian was looking at her, his friend from long ago. He was pleased to see her and yet the sight of her face, it seemed to stab him.

'What about you, are you making ends meet?' she asked.

'Oh aye. Lots of tourists these days hiring boats or wanting tours of the bay. Looking for the Lake Isle of Innisfree and all that shit. 'I will arise and go now!''

They both laughed.

'You'd think it was the only poem that had ever been written!' he said. 'I think they half expect me to arise and recite it!'

They laughed again.

'Maybe you should recite it whilst walking on water. That would impress them.'

He finished the contents of his glass and asked,

'Are you with the girl's dad, then?'

'Yes. No wedding though, who would I have invited?'

Brian nodded.

'What about you?' she asked.

'What has a family ever been to me?'

Now it was Kate's turn to nod in silent recognition of a truth.

'Actually, do you have any wine?' she asked.

◆

Brian returned from the kitchen with a bottle.

He opened it with a corkscrew

'At least you've a corkscrew.'

'What do you mean?'

'The other night I opened a bottle with the screw-driver she used to remove the lock from the bathroom door that night she went mad. Do you remember?'

She drank some of the wine and almost spat it out.

'Jesus! What is this shit?'

'You didn't used to be so fussy. Do you want it or not?'

'Do you remember all those bottles of Hirondelle we used to drink, sitting freezing in the sand dunes?'

That was the last summer there before Kate and her words sailed the high seas on a longship to a new life.

'I've often wondered if the same thing happened to me that happened to her would I be so angry for years and years on end. It was the embarrassment of loving an outsider and then being deserted. She'd made a mistake and everyone could see it.'

'Do we have to talk about our mothers, Kate? I don't want to remember.'

'Surely you remember anyway. You're here in this house.'

'I do remember, I do,' he said. 'Her grief... I understand it... she needed to be angry with someone. She wanted to punish me. But she didn't need to. I used my own anger against myself.'

'Do you still sleep in that room?'

'Yes.'

'God, Brian. With the empty bed beside you?'

'To be honest, Kate, you know I dread every night yet every morning I've no recollection of getting into bed.'

'You don't need to punish yourself, Brian. Surely you can talk to someone who can help?'

'It's too late for all that.'

'It's never too late, Brian…there's lots of possibilities…'

'Everything got shut down then, Kate. What have I ever been since that day?'

She couldn't speak and made do with drinking her wine.

Brian took out his cigarettes and lit up.

'Want one?'

'No, I gave up.'

He was as thin as a rake and his hands shook when he held the lighter to his cigarette but even the sight of his grey stubble made her fall in love with his vulnerability all over again.

She poured herself another glass of wine.

Brian picked up the bottle and poured some wine into the pint glass that had held the Guinness.

'Is this the only bottle?' Kate asked.

'Are you planning to make a night of it?'

A look passed between them that made her a bit worried.

'Lavinia's at the gig at the hotel. I need to get back for her at some point.'

'Do you ever listen to Springsteen these days?'

Brian asked.

'I'm only allowed to listen to that strange stuff that Lavinia has on her iPad. It's all so blatant and aggressive. Sex and the f word. That was our taboo then. Where will songs go now that that taboo has been broken?'

He swished through the device on a docking station until the sound of 'Independence Day' could be heard, with its anguished ache of regret of the broken relationship. Yet there was a note of longing in it, a last note of longing. It was almost unbearable to listen to, with its crushing realisation that even if time had brought understanding, nothing could really change. It was too late.

They'd listened to that song obsessively the summer before she left, feeding money into the jukebox in the pub. Often drunk, the pair of them, and beyond their mothers' reach now that anger had thrust independence upon them. Brian no home to go to. And Kate unwilling to go home now that her mother's domain had become an autocracy, a kingdom of rage, and Kate its only subject and its only object.

For a few years she had tried to use logic to dispel her mother's bitter complaints, quietly stating her case against the escalating illogicality of her mother's argument with life itself, until eventually all light and logic were devoured by her mother's rage.

Sometimes Kate did go back to that house of darkness, defiantly drunk and exercising her right not to be controlled, to be a free spirit, even if her spirit was troubled.

And when her mother screamed at her 'Are you drunk again?' Kate would push past her and scream 'Fuck you!'

That was the level to which political debate had sunk in this republic of discord.

She had become a dissident.

◆

Brian went to the drawer and took a packet of tobacco and rolling papers out and on the little table he rolled a joint. He lit it up and smoked.

'Want some?'

'Fuck! Go on then. For old time's sake.'

There seemed no point in resisting the pressure of the past. She might as well give into it now and start again in the morning.

She dragged on the joint and inhaled it deeply.

They passed it between them a couple of times. She allowed her head to come to rest on the back of the sofa.

The last summer; Brian and Kate, two lonely curlews crying on a dystopian beach. Even the sea seemed to weep with them, flinging cold salty spray into their faces. Frozen and half-drunk she dreamed of Paris and the Café de la Paix where she would sit with Thérèse Desqueroux. Together they would drink their first glass of freedom at a table on the pavement in front of the café. And together they would make a toast to escape from the oppression of a poisonous family.

At first she had tried migration, returning each spring or autumn, brought back by a tide controlled by some dark angry moon. In her absence her mother seemed to understand that it was her own anger that had driven Kate away but she was powerless to control it, and was by turns angry, regretful, then angry again, push, pull, push, leaving Kate tossed about like the shingle, battered by a violent tide.

So the visits became sporadic. Like gunfire.

Then exile the only answer.

Uprooted from her landscapes, her homeland, her people, for a few years she had been infected by her mother's darkness.

And for a few years she went from bed to bed looking for a new home.

◆

Brian came over and sat beside her. He put his lips to hers and started to kiss her. His arms were sinewy and strong, his skin leathery from salt and windburn. She wanted to put her lips to his neck and drink in his saltiness. It was amazing how even after all this time she still had those feelings for him. A sort of brotherhood of the damaged ones.

If Kate and Thérèse Desqueyroux met again in

their exile, and Thérèse, turning philosophical after too many cigarettes and a bottle of Pouilly, asked, what did it matter to love one country or another, Kate would answer that it did matter, your first country, that was your soul and how could your soul fit into somewhere else? A soul was not made of plasticine, it could not be moulded.

And as they drank, Thérèse might then ask, if their lives were indeed a filthy river emanating from a pure source, how was it that the river had been sullied?

Kate thought now what had not occurred to her when she was young. That exile was all very well if there was wine and Paris, but what they had done to Thérèse was to exile her from her child.

At this thought, Kate pulled herself away from Brian.

'God, Brian, I can't do this. I don't want to fuck it all up again. I worked so hard to make it good.'

She started to cry and tried to stand up.

'Don't go,' he said. 'You can't know what it's like to have you here. You're like salt in my wound, but I want it, I want it. If you can't love me, can you cut me, Kate, and rub salt in it? I want you to hurt me. I want the pain of it all to be real. Every time I am out on that boat I see his face looking up at me but I can't get him, he's just below the surface, drowning. And it's the same in my dreams, no matter how much I drink I cannot drown that memory with drink nor can I reach him. It's him I'm dreaming about, but I'm the one who's drowning. I wake up, drowning.'

'Brian,' she said. 'Brian. I felt so guilty leaving you.'

For a few moments they sat side by side on the sofa in silence, his boney fingers clinging on to her hands, their heads touching.

'I felt guilty leaving my homeland…'

'Let's just drink the wine and let us find some peace in each other's company.'

'….walking away from it all.'

'You were right to go.'

Darkness descended on them, unnoticed, as they sat in silent consideration of what had been wasted, what lost.

Was this fragmentary moment all there was to be by way of reconciliation with the past?

The past. It was catching up with her again, de-stabilising her. She didn't want it to. It was time for Kate to get out of there. Even if she had to return from time to time to feed the dark side of her soul.

◆

She took a chair outside the farmhouse to sit in the peace of the spring morning and take in the view. The sun was rising over the quiet cottages, lighting up the yellow gorse lining the lane like lights on a runway. Well, she didn't really want to consider the view, she wanted to have it there as a backdrop while she read over the notes she'd been making as she worked her way through her father's dictionary.

Lavinia came out of the door, scanning the lanes for a sight of Enda. He and Lavinia had spent the last week out walking together. She went back inside and brought another chair and sat it down beside Kate.

'Are you working on your poem?' she asked, zipping up her jacket over her chin.

'It's not a poem,' Kate replied.

'What is it, then?'

'Well, it's a, well, I don't know, a sort of … rumination.'

'Rumination?'

'What's wrong with that?'

'Nothing….'

'Why don't you just read it?' said Kate, passing the notebook to Lavinia.

'No. You read it to me.'

'Read it to you?'

'Yeah! Like when you told me 'Sing it yourself'. You sing it yourself.'

'Ok but you promise you won't laugh?'

'No,' said Lavinia, yawning.

Kate took a breath and prepared to read. She was strangely nervous. She cleared her throat and began.

'Let us consider the complex…'

'Let us consider?' interjected Lavinia.

'Yes. If that is how I want to begin, that is how I will begin.'

Lavinia sighed, placed her face in the palms of her hands, as if to concentrate better.

'Let us consider the complex nature of a word, even a simple word. To consider everything that a word contains, even a short word, such as the word 'word': a meaning, an intent, a conveyance, a signal. The immense power of even a single word. Never mind the role that a word plays in a sentence, and the sentences on a page. Just the word itself. Its history and the changes that a word can undergo. The many different places a word has been, geographically or grammatically or metaphorically; its declensions and tenses, its singularities, pluralities or clauses. Every word is in itself a poem.'

'Is this where all your dictionary reading has brought you?' said Lavinia.

'You asked me to sing. This is me singing,' answered Kate and she smoothed the pages of the notebook and carried on.

'Words are as complex as people. Words are like our genes. They enable us to perpetuate ourselves. They preserve us from oblivion. They are continuous. They are passed down to the next generation through families. They contain our histories. They tell our stories, our stories are written in them. Like genes, words give instructions. They can send the right or wrong message. Like genes, words mutate. The mutation of words, that is etymology. Etymology comes from the Greek word 'etumos' meaning 'true'. And words are true even when they aren't the truth or when they are used to tell lies. Words are like music. They sing!'

'They sing!' cried Lavinia, laughing. 'They sing!'

'They are infinite in number. Their source is not from a unique point, like humans they are pooled from many countries. But they are essentially of humanity, they are essential to humanity. Words are human. We are made up of them. They are alive. They live in us. We carry words around in us from place to place; on long-ships, pilgrim ships, on coffin ships and convict ships. And as the words travel, crossing surreptitiously over borders, like a movement of refugees, the words flour-ish, they collect more words. Words have histories. Words have roots. Their history is held in the word itself, the way the past is still held and has meaning in our present lives. But words are always changing. They are fluent and shifting. They mingle with each other. And they go forth into the world and form new units, like families. And a family of words, that is a language. A language is a melting pot of words from different sources, spoken by a people with ideas or illusions of homogeneity. Some words, like some humans, fare better than others. Some are more popular, some are given more respect. Who can ever say how or why. Some live longer than others. A word, like a human, may die. But like humanity, words will never die. But no matter how much a word changes over time, in meaning or in spelling, the root of the word remains the same and you cannot go back and change it. The past still has its tale to tell, its influence, and you can look backwards down the long line of a word's history but you cannot travel backwards to the root. Who knows when the first human was born, or when first the sound of a mere utterance became a word.'

Lavinia looked at her mother's face for a moment before speaking.

'Is this what you do when I'm not around?' she asked.

'And all this time there was you thinking that I was just your mummy,' said Kate.

'Where does all this come from?' Lavinia asked.

Kate hesitated a moment.

'From here.'

◆

The house behind them was empty now of possessions. Brian had offered to pick them up and drive them along the bumpy road to the airport. Kate imagined how the three of them would have to sit up front, the suitcases tucked in between their legs, the last of the bin bags bouncing around in the back of the truck. She hoped the time would be in their favour, when the alcohol levels in his body from the night before were starting to wear off but before he started his day's drinking.

Lavinia stood up – she'd spotted Enda at the bottom of the lane. He hung back a little, unsure of himself and a little self-effacing, possibly afraid of Kate. Lavinia ran down the lane towards him.

Kate brought to mind her list of Viking words and wondered if she could turn them into a few lines about her own life. The thought amused her. It suited her to be a Viking. And if she were a Viking, this would be her tale.

Freckled kid haunted by mistakes. Her saga of bleak hell. In a mire of anger she snubbed her roots. She chose to take the rotten dregs. How weak!

Kate watched Enda put his arm around her beautiful daughter. Any minute now he would be telling her how he loved her pilgrim soul. It was their goodbye walk. Better a goodbye than a lifetime of discord. In her mind's eye, Kate took up her pen and wrote the last line of her Viking tale.

Bairn birth; gift.

Rosemary Johnston

Acknowledgements

Andrew, Abby and Rory - you are always my first inspiration.

Thank you to Sam Ruddock at Story Machine for enabling this book to see the light of day, and for his gently guiding editorial hand which has made the book a richer piece of work.

Thank you for supporting planet-friendly publishing

Story Machine seeks to have a net positive social and environmental impact. That means the environment and people's lives are actually better off for every book we print. Story Machine offsets our entire carbon footprint plus 10% through a www.ClimateCare.org programme. We are now investing in converting to use only 100% renewable energies and seeking out the most planet-positive means of shipping books to our readers.

The printing insustry is a huge polluter, requiring the use of huge amounts of water, toxic chemicals, and energy. Even FSC certified mix paper sources drive deforestation. That's why we are proud to be working with Seacourt, a global leader in planet positive printing. Not only have they developed a waterless and chemical-free process, they use only 100% renewable energies, FSC certified recycled paper, and direct absolutely no waste to landfill. That's why they were crowned Europe's most sustainable SME in 2017, and have been recognised as one of the top three environmental printers in the world.

Planet-positive printing costs us a little more. But we think this is a small price to pay for a better world, today and in the future. If you agree, please share our message, and encourage other publishers and authors to commit to planet-positive printing. Stories can change the world. They deserve publishers that want to make sure they do. Together, we can make publishing more sustainable.